I AM Human Too Part Two Of Three Parts(The Love Games) By Ane M

I Am Human Too: My Blood

The Love games, Volume 2

Ane M

Published by Ane.M, 2023.

This is a work of fiction. Similarities to real people, places, or events are entirely coincidental.

I AM HUMAN TOO: MY BLOOD

First edition. December 5, 2023.

Copyright © 2023 Ane M.

ISBN: 979-8224112111

Written by Ane M.

Also by Ane M

Billionaire For The Holidays
Billionaire For The Holidays

The Love games
I Am Human Too (Rain Again)
I Am Human Too: My Blood
I Am Human Too: Never Ever
I Am Yours: Love In Full Bloom
I Am Yours: Between The Lines

Table of Contents

To Anethemba Mnqumevu

Great things aren't accomplished in a day. You have to fight for them every single second of the hour you're existing.

I AM Human Too

The Love Games Book One

Ane M

1

Part Two: My Blood

About The Book

Obsession is not love. But it is a toxin that kills someone ever so slowly.

Sandra finds out about this the hard way. She was obsessed with her brother's mate, her brother's soulmate thinking that it was love. She did everything in her power to win Josh's love but to no avail because Josh only loved Max.

Blood is supposed to be thicker than water but in this case the two siblings are fighting over the love of another.

After the tragic events of the past, Max and Josh are working to rebuild their lives together. But their happiness is threatened by a new threat - the obsessive love Zinzi feels for her brother's mate, Zakhi. Zinzi has always hated her brother Babalo. Balz is unaware of Zinzi's true feelings for him, but if he discovers the truth, it could tear their family apart. Will Max and Josh be able to protect Balz and Zakhi from Zinzi's dangerous love, or will they all be trapped in a never-ending cycle of tragedy?

If you're looking for a story of love and obsession, then "I AM HUMAN TOO: MY BLOOD" is the book for you. Filled with suspense and drama, this novel will keep you on the edge of your seat. Zinzi's twisted affection for her brother's mate threatens to destroy everything in its path, and only Max and Josh can save the day. Pick up a copy of this thrilling novel today and join the adventure!

Chapter One: All is forgotten

Balz got woken up by something shaking him. He groaned still wanting to sleep more. But the shaking got even more persistent. He angrily opened his eyes ready to snap at the person brave enough to wake a sleeping lion. The minute he opened his eyes though his anger turned into confusion. Confusion of seeing Zakhi in front of him. Confusion of seeing the unfamiliar room he was in.

" Beu!" Zakhi's voice made him snap out of it.

" Zakhi? Am I dreaming?" He really was unsure if this was reality. Especially when he saw the position they both were in.

" I wish I could say you were but you aren't now you're beginning to be too heavy for me. Plus I am very hungry now. I think you are too so if you'd kindly let go of my neck"

Balz saw what Zakhi was talking about. His arms were tightly wrapped around Zakhi's neck. He bit his lip asking himself why he didn't feel like letting go. Why he didn't have it in him to let go of the guy he had called names,insulted and just been downright mean to almost their whole lives. He really wanted to ask himself to let go but he couldn't get himself to. He felt like he could stay like that for an internity.

" Beu? Are you still there?" Zakhi snapped his fingers at him.

" What's Beu?" He decided to ask Zakhi. Just to stall sometime.

" Beu is what I call you" Zakhi answered simply.

" That's not what I'm asking dumb person! I'm asking you why you call me 'Beu' " Zakhi inhaled deeply putting both his hands on Balz's back. Which made Balz bite his lower lip even more at the sensation those hands made on him. " I call you Beu because it's short for Beautiful, that being short for —" he was stopped from his sentence when he heard Balz's gasp

" Beautiful? You think I'm beautiful?" The vulnerability in his voice as he asked those questions made Zakhi's heart ache horribly. Did Balz really think of himself so poorly? That he had to have someone else confirm his beauty.

He didn't let that emotion slip though. He smiled gently at the foolish guy on top of him. He raised his hand gently brushing Balz's forehead. " I don't think, I know you're beautiful. And you should know that as well. Duh? Why do you think so many girls fall for you?" He was talking about something he knew. He had seen a lot of girls with Balz, a lot of girls crying over him because he didn't give them the time of day. Probably because he spent so much of his time plotting schemes of messing with Zakhi. " And you didn't let me finish, I call you Beu because you're a sleeping Beauty"

Balz pouted at that part, " I'm a sleeping beauty? " " Why would you call me that?" Zakhi continued brushing Balz's forehead. " You're sleeping beauty because you always seem to find a chance to sleep everytime you're on my arms. And you look so cute sleeping. Very cute. " Balz felt his face heat up at 'cute'. He really didn't know what Zakhi was doing to him and all he knew was it was messing with his head. A lot. After a few minutes of coaching himself he finally pried his arms from around Zakhi's neck.

" Now about that food" Zakhi smiled at the mention of food. He sat up with Balz still in his arms. Now he was sitting on top of his lap. But he didn't mind since it wasn't the first time. To say the truth he'd gotten used to Balz's weight on him. " You want to go to the kitchen? Or should I just bring it here for you?"

Balz's took sometime to think about it. This wasn't his house so he couldn't be comfortable at someone's bedroom. " Mhmm, let's go to the kitchen" Zakhi nodded smiling. " You should get off me though. I don't think you want me to carry you again. Now would you?"

That image of Zakhi carrying him all the way from Zinzi's car to the inside of the house not stopping there he even carried him to his bedroom. It messed with Balz's already messed up head. The tingles he felt only made it worse, he wasn't the lightest if ever like he mentioned he worked out a lot. So Zakhi must have had a hard time.

" And your sister says I'm the mind wonderer, I'm seeing that you escape to your mind a lot" Zakhi said as he gently put Balz on the bed.

" I wasn't kidding about being hungry you know" that only served to make Balz feel even more guilter.

" Come on let's go and eat" Zakhi grabbed his arm to help him stand. They both stood in front of each other staring at one another. Their moment was broken when Zakhi's alarm went off. " 20:32, my eat time. So let's not waste time."

Balz laughed at the fact that Zakhi actually sets his eating times. Foolish person. He allowed himself be dragged down by Zakhi not that he minded. He found out he liked Zakhi's hand on his. They blended and fit each other so well.

When they finally reached the kitchen he was disappointed to feel Zakhi slip his warm hand away from his own. " Since I can't cook anything... anything but eggs that's what we're gonna eat"

" I think it's my turn to cook now. I mean you've done so much for me already. Plus I also don't know how to cook anything but eggs"

Zakhi wanted to argue but the determined look on his eyes told him he wouldn't win a fight against him now. So he simply nodded. " I'll get you the pot, cooking spray and not forgetting the eggs"

Balz didn't know what he was doing wrong. All the eggs, he'd made so far were burnt and really uneatable. He groaned at the severely burnt egg he'd made.

" Ug! I give up" he said putting his hands on his face. Hands that were removed from his face by Zakhi.

" Now, that's not the Balz I know. " Zakhi took the burnt egg tasting a little piece from it. " See it isn't that bad but you can do better. I know you can"

" But I'm gonna do it by myself right now because I'm hungrrrrrrrry". Balz's couldn't stay grumpy with Zakhi around making him laugh. Balz went to sit on one of the kitchen's barstools. Watched as Zakhi went to his work. With an onion and a knife on his hand. " I like eggs mixed with onion" he explained himself but turned to look at Balz again. " You do eat onion with eggs right?"

" Never ate it before but I'm open to new things". Balz looked at all the process Zakhi went to as he chopped the onion into the thinest slices, then the way he mixed the five eggs on one bowl. Precisely stirring at it. It was only a good wonder to see the beautiful results.

" Let's dig in" Zakhi said placing a plate in front of Balz. They ate for five minutes before they were done. Zakhi took their plates and put them on the dishwasher. His aunt was a lot of things and lazy was one of them. She'd rather have a machine to wash the dishes than ruin her nails. Not that Zakhi had any complaints.

" Let's go to sleep" he told the yawning Balz.

And he refuses being Sleeping Beauty.

The next morning...

Balz woke up feeling cold. His eyes shot up. Seeing exactly why he was cold. Zakhi wasn't in bed. He sat up on the bed. Stretching his arms. " Zakhi?" He called out but got no response. He decided to get up from bed. Searching for Zakhi. Maybe he was in the bathroom.

He went to open the bathroom door only to see Zakhi getting out of the shower. Naked! He just froze. Not knowing what to do next but just stare at the well made man just inches from him. When Zakhi's eyes landed to his, he quickly turned. Looking at the bed instead.

" Beu you're awake" Zakhi said wrapping a towel around himself. " You should shower too. It's almost time for school"

Balz nodded. Still not turning to look at Zakhi who walked in the room. Ramanging inside his closet for his shirt and pants. " I'll borrow you some of mine today" he said putting the shirt and pants on the unmade bed.

Balz went to shower. Asking himself why he was getting the kinds of emotions he did now around Zakhi. Zakhi was still the guy he'd grown up hating. Still the guy who... felt like he'd wronged.

They got to school by foot since Zakhi didn't have a car. Not that he never owned one because he did. A whole lot of them . The only problem was he couldn't keep one. Always caused an accident with them. He always drove too fast or too slow. So he just gave up on the whole thing entirely. Cars were not for him.

Balz had laughed at him when he told him that.

" We have the same classes in the morning right?" He asked as both he and Zakhi got inside the school. Zakhi nodded.

There had been chatting and noise but when they walked in that all stopped. Everyone's eyes on them.

" They're alive" one said breaking the silence. And that was all the others needed to get on speaking mode. Pats and shoulder hugs. Were given to the both of them. ' Welcome back' from all the people Balz and Zakhi never thought would actually care if they lived or died.

" Baby! " Zinzi ran to Zakhi. A sloppy kiss on his mouth. And a hug that didn't sit well with Balz. So much so that he went and broke them apart.

" This is a school. Not a making out place for you two" he said with hands folded angrily in front of him. He wasn't jealous! Just didn't like to see his sister with his biggest enemy. Enemy? Yes that's what Zakhi was to him not a friend. But Enemy!

He pulled Zakhi to the further side from everyone else. " Zakhi... Zakhile listen and listen good what happened yesterday and the previous days we've been together stays between us. No one can know that I was actually nice to you. No one can know about anything that happened between us clear?" Zakhi knew it would be like this. Not that he minded. But he'd still miss the nice , funny and adorable Balz.

" Alright Beu...Balz... Babalo...Nah I'll still call you Beu. Everything else though is history. All is forgotten. "

Balz's felt a pang of something in his gut at the way Zakhi said that . So casually, too uncaring. Just like how he wanted it. Then why did it make him feel so bad?

Zinzi heard everything. What had happened between her brother and boyfriend? That Balz would actually not want to talk about it to any one. What was so huge that no one could know about? Was it what she was thinking? Did Balz and Zakhi do something? Something that could destroy her relationship with her brother and boyfriend? Did they actually do what she feared most?

The ringing of the bell signalling for the start of the day changed her thoughts into the thoughts of homework she hadn't done.

Oh my God! Miss Sharlot is going to kill me!

Chapter Two: Dream on

BALZ WAS BACK TO HIS old self again. Throwing insults at Zakhi but not as gruesome as before. They actually were very tamed than before.

" Are you going easy on him?" Litha asked as Balz ate his lunch at breaktime. Balz who had taken a slice of sandwich to his mouth and didn't really understand what his sidekick was asking him. " Let me elaborate, you've been insulting him with weak things like ' You're so ugly or were you born that way?' Dude that's tamed for you" Balz swallowed his food and looked at Litha. " Tamed? My insults are weak? Boy had my being lost in the jungle made you step up to me? What I do, say and don't say is all my choice and has nothing to do with you understand?" Lit nodded. " Understood" " Good now get out of my face. I want to eat alone"

Lit walked away. Anger radiating inside of him. He hated the way Balz treated him and Fox.

" Dude let it go. He's always been like that, rude to us. What's different today? " Fox asked him.

" What's different today is that I want a change I am tired of being a side kick. He gets to decide who we're enemies with and gets to decide whether or not we're mean to them. No thank you. I want to be my own leader now. And the only way is to take him out of the game" His eyes filled with menace. Scaring Fox. He'd never seen his friend like this. Never.

M ax stood in front of Zinzi's locker. Waiting for her to finally finish cheering squad practice. It was long wait but he had the time and patience.

When she finally walked out with a couple of girls he suspected were her friends. They came to a stop at his presence Zinzi's brow furrowed. " Can I have a word with you?" he asked ever so gentlemanly. The girls beside Zinzi giggled and walked away understanding this had nothing to do with them.

" So what do you want to talk about?" she asked the new kid who was kind of creeping her out. I mean she did not know him, not to talk of well enough for him to actually be standing in front of her locker. Asking her to have a word. A word? What the hell was it? Nineteen sixty?!

" I've been looking at you for a while and I'm starting to like you" well that came all of a sudden. " Excuse me?" she wanted to be sure that she'd heard the guy correctly. She hadn't been hitten on ever since she and Zakhi got together. So she didn't really remember how to approach things like this anymore. " You heard me. So how about it? Wanna go out with me?"

Who the hell was this guy?!

" No, guy listen I know you're new here and you don't really know whose with who. So let me explain it for you. I am off limits. I'm Zakhi's girlfriend"

Max made a shocked face at that. " You mean Zakhi? Zakhile? The one that's with Balz?"

Zinzi's heart quickened at that . " Balz?! Why would you think that?!". " My boyfriend isn't gay!!!"

" Uh? He isn't then why do I always see him one way or another in Balz's company? Or is it friendship is that it?"

Zinzi was getting frustrated by the questions Max was asking her. Frustrated because these were the same questions she asked herself every single day.

" Here put your numbers, I want to call you tonight" Max said handing her his phone.

Zinzi looked at the phone only to see the wallpaper. Balz's on Zakhi's chest. With Zakhi's lips going for a kiss on his forehead. Zinzi let the phone slip to the floor. " What?! What is this?"

" That my dear is your boyfriend with his boyfriend... sorry your brother" " Now if you change your mind about getting out with me give me a call. Okay?" he returned Zinzi's phone to her. A phone she didn't realize she had given to him.

He picked up his own from the floor.

" Balz and Zakhi are together face it sweetly crafted angel. There's only I who wants you."

" Dream on! Balz is my brother I know him better than anyone he'd never do something to hurt me. Never with my boyfriend. So what you're saying now is absolutely lies!"

" Am I? Zinzi ask yourself one thing what really happened in that camping trip. You weren't there but I was. I saw everything happen in front of my eyes. You should have seen them how they loved to be alone together doing what God knows what. And then just like that disappeared. Why only them? I was in their team why didn't I disappear with them?"

" I don't know! Maybe you all split up or something"

" If we did really split up why were they still together? I'm telling you they're fooling you. The sooner you accept that the better. "

Chapter Three: What if?

BALZ GOT INTO CLASS. Math class wasn't really his strong suit so he'd rather sit up in the back and not answer anything. The teacher Miss Nirt was already used to that. So it wouldn't make any difference now.

" Today I am giving you assignments each. These assignments you will either choose by yourselves if you want a partner or not. I expect them back Monday morning. " The whole class groaned at that. The woman wanted them to have a Math assignment! Done in only three days. Others had a life. People like Balz. He had to attend several parties at the weekend. So why was this teacher ruining his plans now?

" Baby will you be my partner?" he heard his sister ask Zakhi. They were right in front of his desk so he could see and hear both of their interactions.

" I wish I could but I already have a partner sweetheart" he kissed her cheek to console her. Balz let it process in his head. If Zakhi wouldn't partner with Zinzi then who? Could it be that Max guy? They had seemed friendly enough but Max wasn't in this class with them.

He was so deep in his thoughts that he didn't feel anyone sitting next to him on the vacant seat next to him. That was until the other cleared his throat.

He turned to see who it was. He was surprised to see the kid from the camp. " Hi"

" Hey" he greeted back warmly. " How you doing?" he felt a little guilty for still not knowing his name even now.

" I'm fine. Just got back to school. I heard you just did too. Something about you and Zakhile missing" he didn't really like this type of topic. Not just because it brought back memories of him wondering around hungry but it also brought back memories of him and Zakhi. How Zakhi had taken care of him the whole way there. How he'd catch him every time he tripped or fell.

" Yeah that. So about you again did they find out how you got the poisoning?" Balz thought it was a little odd that everyone ate the same thing in the camp but didn't get sick or poisoned.

The guy was about to answer when a shadow suddenly casted itself in front of them. Balz looked up only to see it was Zakhi's huge form and on the right side Max's. He didn't know why Max was in the class or why he was giving the kid he was talking to the stare down. But what really puzzled him most was the way Zakhi was looking at him. Almost like jealous boyfriend kind of way.

Whoa Zakhi was jealous about Balz talking to his...uh! He had to know the kid's name. He was about to ask just that before the kid got rudely pulled out the door by Max.

Zakhi on the other hand folded his hands. " Your place or mine" Balz was taken back by this question.

Why would Zakhi just suddenly ask me that?

Hadn't he been clear this morning that all their ' friendliness' should be dissolved. What was happening now?

" I asked you a question. Where are we doing the project your place or mine?" Project? When did he agree to be Zakhi's partner? He would have stated that matter factly if Zakhi didn't give him a fright with his stare. He looked like he wanted no excuses or reasons for not being his partner. Fine then. He sucked at this subject anyway. Why not level his code one into a three.

" My place. "

Zakhi nodded. " I'll be there at seven"

That seemed a little late. " No how about we get started on it after school?"

" I've got some errands to do first,so it's seven or eight in the morning tomorrow" okay he liked the late part more now.

" See you then" he smiled awkwardly at Zakhi who didn't show any expression to him. Just walked away to his desk next to Zinzi.

Who gave him a quiz face. And then shot one to Balz too. As if he was responsible to making Zakhi all grumpy.

Had he said something? Nah. Nothing to have made Zakhi that angry. He had actually not even been nasty to Zakhi all since they came back home.

M ax got pushed to the wall. Sometimes he forgot Josh's true strength. But he wouldn't stand down and let Josh out of it this time.

" What the hell was that?!" Josh exclaimed his deep graspy voice making as if there was a thunderstorm in the boys bathroom. " Do you know how stupid that was?! You could have almost blown our cover!"

" I don't care about the cover when it comes to us. When it comes to you and I. I give no shit of this mission or our reason of being here. " Josh sighed looking away from him. " No! Josh you will not look away from me! Not today. Today I've got to tell you that I hate the way you look at Balz. We're here to bring him and Zakhi together not for you to start falling for him yourself"

" Control yourself" Josh said still not looking at Max's direction. " We are here to complete a mission. Of course I'm gonna have to play the character that I was assigned to. "

" Was your character assigned to act as if he's in love with Balz?! Was it? No! You're doing all this yourself"

" Was your character assigned to be acting like he loves Zinzi was it? No! You're doing that on your own and I haven't said anything!" Josh spat back.

" Ohh! This is about that? Revenge? I am trying to get her out of the way so Balz and Zakhi can get closer together. The sooner they're together the better. "

Josh looked at him suspiciously. " And what's the rush? They have all this year to fall in love. And they're already bonding so why do you have to rush the process?"

" Because! I... nevermind. We are here to do the job not lose each other. Please I'm begging you Josh don't cheat on me. Especially now. Please it will do so much damage"

Josh looked at him for real this time. Only now starting to realize Max's eyes weren't the light blue they usually were but were now mixed with a white colour. Making them look like another colour all together. That was not all in his inspection,he started to look at Max's normal to the humans face but to him,the one who knew him so well he saw that the face was swollen. The rest of his body didn't go untouched in all of this. His hips were wider, he was large, larger than his real size. Some would confuse that largeness as muscle but not Josh. He knew exactly what this meant. And it wasn't good.

" Uh..why do you look.. like.. you're carrying?" he knew the truth already but just had to try.

Maybe Earth food made him big... maybe..

" Josh you know that I am so please don't ask stupid questions. Instead you should be thinking of a solution to this"

" How long?" he asked. Max took his hand and placed it on his stomach. He felt a nuzzle on his hand. He smiled fondly. The baby was already responding to his touch. That was good. It meant he already knew his father. He looked at Max who opened his mouth to speak.

" Three months" he whispered breaking Josh from his moment with the baby.

Josh became frozen. That long! It meant they had no time to waste. They had to finish this mission quickly and run as far away as they could. The others would start smelling the scent soon enough. That got him to the question of why didn't he? Himself smell the scent from his mate.

" I used a repealing substance I took from your mother when we left"

" Whoa! Whoa you knew you were pregnant even when we left to start this mission?! Why didn't you tell me? Do you freakin know how much danger we're in now? The council will know about our relationship. They'll want our heads. Reaping that baby away from us."

" Josh shut the fuck up! What would you have done? You would have refused us going to this mission! You would have made them suspicious of us. Then it would have been so much easier for them to take us out along with our baby but now. Now we get a head start. Earth is a big place,we can raise our baby here. "

" Running? How can a child be raised with always being on the run? Hmm?"

" Josh I am only thinking from my maternal instincts. And they're telling me to protect my baby even from you. If you cheat in anyway it will harm me and our baby. I can't have that. I'd rather be killed by the council than go the way my mother went. I can't! I saw her pain I just..." as he broke down Josh was there holding his trembling body.

" Aus, it will all be fine mate. I promise you. We'll just have to find a way out. To protect you and our little baby. " He placed his hand on the flat stomach of his mate. He felt the nuzzle he'd felt the first time. " He's going to be able to see us both. We'll raise him. Here in Earth. I don't care how many council members they send to kill us. We'll handle them together."

Max smiled into his mate's warm touch. " Sah, I love you mate" he whispered on Josh's ear.

" Love you more Aus" he kissed the top of the temple of his mate.

They stood there in their embrace only until there was a loud knock on the bathroom door.

" Hey! What's going on inside there?! Open up!"

They both heaved sighs. " Humans"

" Let's get this mission finished" Max nodded as they tore away from each other. He started by fixing himself. Wiping the unfallen tears just to wipe away evidence of him being emotional. Pregnancy did this...but above all the fear for his children's lives being at stake..three to be exact. He hadn't told Josh that. And wouldn't be telling him until the later stages. He'd just overreact now.

" Love you" they both said the same time to each other.

One last lingering glances and then they were apart and walking out the door like nothing had happened.

They had to finish the mission and quickly.

Only eight months were left now. Till Max gave birth.

Zinzi and Balz got back home. They were tired from the walk they'd endured all because of Balz' s car not starting.

" You know this is all your fault right?" Zinzi said grumpier than ever. She was just trying to cause a fight with him as always. Usually he'd be more than glad to fight with his sister but not today. Not when Zakhi was coming to his house. Not when Zakhi was coming here.

Not when he had to get ready. Most importantly clean his room. If there's anything he knew about Zakhi it was that he was a neat freak. And Balz's room was a pigsty.

" Mommy! Can I borrow one of the spare rooms?! " he hardly asked anything from his parents. Only spoke when needed to be.

" What my boy?" his mom asked with a confused face. As she appeared from the living room.

" I said can I borrow a spare room today I prefer the ones outside" Their house wasn't small by any convictions. Too big to be a mansion since it had it's own 'spare rooms' from the outside. Which were house big.

" Why?" his mom asked him with a normal mother's concern in her tone. Which just made Balz smile.

" Where was this concern ten years ago?" he muttered under his breath and looked at her straight in the eyes. Knowing she heard him. " I have a friend coming over. He's a neat freak so I can't have him seeing my dirty one. Plus I don't want you all to make fun of my little knowledge of mathematics as we do that project. "

His mom smiled a forced and strained smile. " It's okay. Just don't dirty it up too much."

He nodded as he left. Walking into his own room. Quickly removing his school wear. Only leaving him with his trunks.

Now what to wear?

He felt disgusted at himself for even wanting to dress good for his sister's boyfriend. A guy who probably didn't even feel all these strange emotions he was feeling now.

What got him the most was the fact that Zakhi messed him up so much that he's even considering how being kissed by him would feel. How being touched by him for real would be like. Not just the touching they did. What it would feel like for Zakhi to have emotion in his eyes just for him.

How– Stop it Balz! He's your friend now nothing more!

Then why couldn't he accept that? Why was he getting crazy at just seeing him. Why did it hurt his heart when he saw Zakhi with someone else? The someone else being his sister.

It hadn't bothered you before! He's your sister's boyfriend!

His self-consciousness was fighting with him. And he didn't know who'd win this fight. Himself or it.

Zakhi! Why are you always making my life so difficult? First it was as my enemy but now it's as... friend? What are you doing to me?

Z akhi knocked on the door. He wasn't expecting to be dragged by someone from behind.

When he turned to see who it was he laughed immediately. Balz in an apron. Not just any apron a pink one.

" Wha-what are you wearing?" Balz folded his arms to his chest. Doing the cutest pout face Zakhi had ever seen on a human being.

" Are you angry at me now?" he asked in a baby voice. Getting closer to the big baby in front of him. " What should I do? Hmm? Should I kneel down and apologize? Or should I—" he got even closer to Balz and leaned to his ear and whispered, " Ki—tickle you"

Zakhi almost messed up and said 'kiss' he doesn't know what happens to him when he and Balz meet. When they talk,joke around it always leads to something else. Something neither of them are expecting.

He shook himself. And got a mischievous smile from Balz. He wondered what the pink apron wearing boy was up to.

He felt hands sneakily going up his armpits. Trying to tickle him. He smiled at Balz's ignorance.

" I can't be tickled. Many have tried and failed. Like you are now. "

" But I think I can tickle you instead. It was my idea either way" Balz tried to run away but he was too slow for Zakhi. Who caught him as always. Attacking him with tickles to his sides. They both fell to the grass with him on top of Balz. He laughed so hard that Zakhi thought he'd explode. So he let him go. Getting off him. Landing on the other side of Balz. They lay there on the ground for a while.

Balz sat up still breathing heavily because of the too much laughing. Zakhi stared at him. The way his dark black hair was glistening on the night sky. The moon only increasing to show Balz's beauty. Beauty that just seemed so precious that Zakhi had the urge to protect all for the rest of his life. He didn't even care how weird that sounded. It just felt right to him. He sat up too. His shoulder touching Balz's.

He frowned at seeing Balz's serious face. " What's wrong?" he questioned now a little worried. He had forgotten about Balz's various sicknesses. Maybe he tickled him too much.

" I am thinking" he answered simply.

" Thinking about what?" Zakhi questioned. Wanting to know what the guy who always looked like he didn't think about anything would be possibly thinking about now.

" Zakhi don't get angry but I..uh can I ask you a question?"

Zakhi smiled and nodded. " Why would I get mad for you asking me something?"

" Well uhmm...what if we didn't start out the way we did? What if we could have been friends? What would have happened now? What could have become of us? Would we be the best of friends or–" Zakhi saw that he bit himself to stop speaking. But it was too late. Zakhi could already identify what he was trying to say. He knew it must have been very hard for Balz to have come to ask that question. It only meant that Balz felt the same way as him. That Balz felt the sudden change in their relationship. They weren't enemies anymore. They weren't friends because this kind of relationship they shared now was beyond friendship. Zakhi was afraid to acknowledge this. He also was afraid of answering Balz's questions because they'd just reveal a truth he didn't think he was ready to accept now.

So instead he gave Balz a question of his own. " What if I hadn't been with Zinzi?"

Balz's eyes shot up . " My food!" he quickly got up from the floor and ran to one of the smaller houses that surrounded the main house.

Zakhi got up from the grass as well. Following behind Balz.

Z inzi got away from the tree she had been hiding behind. She didn't know what type of bad luck she had. To have her brother chasing after her boyfriend. It was now obvious. Everything was planned. From the get go. The getting lost. Balz must have planned that. The ' sickness' that had landed him into being unconscious. It was all just an act to get close to her Zakhi.

And this project had to be some plan as well. To trap Zakhi here. With him. It all made sense now. The fussing over clothes, the googling of how certain types of food are cooked.

She can't let him succeed. She had worked too hard herself in order to get Zakhi as her own. She had to do something.. something drastic. But what?

Balz finished serving the both of them. Hoping that the burnt parts of the food wouldn't be visible to Zakhi. He has worked so hard to cook all of this food. And now it would have been ruined all because of the fool he had cooked this food for.

" This is all your fault!" he bursted out to Zakhi. Zakhile who only raised a brow. He was about to let his wrath rain down on the fool when Zakhi spoke.

" Wow! You can cook?"

" Yep. Amazing how Google and a quick learner can do. Very amazing." Balz said praising himself.

" Let's see how it tastes" that was what scared Balz the most. The taste.

" We can order pizza" Balz quickly suggested. He didn't want Zakhi to laugh at him.

" Why? We would be wasting food. You cooked I could never insult your hard work by refusing your food. " That made Balz blush immediately. They both sat on the dinning table and started eating. To Balz the food was good but what he dreaded was that Zakhi would hate it.

" Delicious. You sure you haven't cooked before today? Because you're a natural"

Balz's cheeks went red. " Let's have dessert"

" There's dessert? Beu I'm impressed."

Okay if his cheeks weren't burning him up enough that sure did the trick. He quickly left for the kitchen to go get the cake he had put in the fridge.

He has a smile on his face as he cut it out in slices and put them in both his and Zakhi's plates. But that smile completely fell when he saw his sister on Zakhi's lap both of them in a heated kiss session. His heart felt like it had sank into the deepest parts of his soul.

He cleared his throat. To show them his presence. " Cake, just for you both" he placed the two slices on the table and left to the first bedroom he could find in the guest room.

How could this day go bad? It had been fine just moments ago. So what went wrong now? When did Zinzi even get in the house? Why? Why did she have to ruin...what? What was she ruining?

Him and Zakhile had no relationship of whatsoever. They had nothing. They couldn't be anything but nothing. Zakhile didn't feel what he felt. Zakhi's heart was with Zinzi.

Chapter Four: Good looking

MAX STOOD IN FRONT of the bathroom mirror. Looking at himself. His face was becoming too blown. He lifted up his t-shirt to see his stomach. It hadn't grown yet. Just his packs had disappeared, showing that it would grow soon enough.

He touched it, gently brushing it and humming along with the wind that blew outside.

" You'll survive. You'll be with me. I am going to give birth to you. No matter what." These three babies wouldn't be like the others before them. Sandra was not here to keep them away from him. Sandra wasn't here to blackmail or make him do anything stupid enough to hurt his children. These children he'd protect with his all. These children he'd raise with Josh.

When he got back to the bedroom he got Josh getting in the room. " Hey, you look mad what's up?" he asked as Josh sat with a grumpy attitude on the bed.

" They were so close! And then that Zinzi came out of nowhere. That stupid girl!"

" Hey don't call her that. "

Jealousy quickly shot up on Josh as he stood up immediately pressed Max to the wall.

" Why do you care about her? What she to you?"

" Number one you treating me like this stops today. This is not Zeit planet. You do not rule over me here. You'll hurt my baby if this continues. Number two just because things aren't going per your plan it does not mean that everyone is at fault. Zinzi is just a girl. A girl who thinks she's in love. In love with someone that cannot be hers. She's just like my sister. This story is just like ours except this one I'll make sure it doesn't end up like ours. We have to make sure they're together but the right way. We will not hurt Zinzi in anyway."

" We didn't hurt Sandra, she's insane"

" Yes she might be but we contributed a lot to that. If we had maybe done things differently we could have.." Josh stopped him from continuing by putting his hand on his lips.

" We didn't do anything wrong in loving each other. We didn't do anything wrong by being mates. Max your sister is mad and she deserves to be told that" he took Max's hand into his. Looking up to his eyes. " I love you and you love me. That's all that matters."

Max wishes he could believe that. He really does. He wishes he could trust Josh as he did before but after three miscarriages. He didn't.

" If it was all that matters you wouldn't have cheated on me with her everytime I got pregnant. If it was all that matters then my three babies would be still here now" with that said he pushed himself away from his mate.

" Whoa...what did you say? All the time you got pregnant... three babies? What are you talking about Max?"

Max let free the tears he had been holding for so long. " The first time we made love. At my fifteen birthday I got pregnant with our first child. I wanted to tell you but then I lost it. The day when you slept with Sandra I lost my first child, then it was when I was sixteen when I lost our second child it was because of you cheating on me again,my third miscarriage was when you cheated on me right in front of my eyes. So when I say love isn't enough I mean it. "

Josh tried to come hold him but he raised his hand to stop him. " I need a moment to myself. So I'm going for a walk."

J osh closed his eyes. Gods! How could he have been so stupid? He has broken the trust of his mate. He has been responsible for murdering three of his children! Three!

No wonder Max was so moody and distant towards him. He was the cause of it.

Sandra curse you! You devil!

No. He wouldn't let her win. Not now. Max and him have been through enough and they'll have to go through this too. He'll find a way to heal Max's wounds. No matter what it takes. He'll do it.

M onday morning...

A t highschool this time everything was a buzz. Everyone was busy with asking each other for the matric ball that would come just in two days. All these people were not Balz. He was literally miserable. The energy from the others just making him even more worse.

" Boss man. Long time no see." He saw Lit in front of him. Which only meant that he had to speak and do something but he didn't want to order anyone around today. He just wanted peace and quiet.

" I have to get to class" he told him passing the other boy. He was so down today. He had to just get through today. Anyhow he could. He couldn't afford to miss examination.

When he got to class he saw the face he wasn't ready to see just yet. Zakhi's. He tried to look away immediately but Zakhi already saw him. He walked to his desk only to see a note on top of it. He sat down reading it.

《 Listen I am not good at this... friendship simply because I don't have none. But you're starting to be my friend now. I don't want to lose you as that. So whatever I did I apologise for it. Forgive and forget》

H e raised his head only to see Zakhi looking at him. " So what do you say? Forgive and forget?"

Balz thought about this for a little while. There wasn't anything to forgive or forget. Because Zakhi did nothing wrong. He only kissed his girlfriend nothing more.

But it hurt Balz either way. It was now that he just came with the confirmation that he really, absolutely loved Zakhi. He really did. With all of his heart seeing him with his sister now just triggered something in him. Something worse than jealousy. Self-pity. That was what he was feeling right now. Pity for himself.

Still that did not stop him from forcing a smile for Zakhi." Forgive and forget"

Zakhi smiled. " Good because I thought I'd have to go on my knees and grovel now. And I would if that would make you happy. "

You see! These are the reasons Balz's heart thinks Zakhi loves him as well. Because of the things he says and does. It just broke his heart more that Zakhi didn't even know he was doing this to him.

" Today I'm going tuxedo shopping. Aunt ordered me to, so would you mind coming with me after school? I promise I'll treat you to ice cream"

Ice cream. Now how could he refuse?

" You cheat! Why would you bribe me with ice cream?"

" Duh? I know you're obsessed with that thing. Since we were little. "

Balz only smiled. Zakhi was really too much. How could he get over this crush now? When he's taking him to places. Was this what this was a simple crush?

Balz hoped it was. Something that would disappear with time. He did not think he'd survive if this continued.

Zinzi saw him again. The new guy. Max. This time he was standing in front of the door to the cafeteria.

She sighed. " What do you want?" Max smiled.

" Well I was just standing here minding my own business but since you asked. I want you to go out with me for the matric ball. " Max said confidently.

" Hayi shame I admire your bravado or is it stupidness? Can't be sure. Jonga Max or whatever they call you sweety I am not into you. Zakhi is the only one for me" Max only smirked.

" Oh really? Then the question should be are you the only one for him. "

" What the hell is that supposed to mean?" Zinzi questioned. Still not feeling quite sure of her brother not trying to steal her man.

" Uyayazi into endithetha ngayo my love don't pretend" That surprised Zinzi. He didn't know that Max could speak Xhosa especially not so well.

" What do you want from me?"

" What I want is simple recognize the truth in front of you. Zakhi and Balz are a sealed deal. Their just messing your life up. Are you really gonna let this good looking guy out of your sights just because of someone who probably doesn't even spend enough time with you"

Zinzi questioned herself. When was the last time she and Zakhi went out somewhere? These days it was either project, getting lost or cooking with Balz. It was never her and him. That had to stop. Today!

Zakhi could not tell the difference between the two tuxedos in Balz's hands.

" What did you say was wrong with this one again?" he asked holding the red one he chose first before Balz took it to himself to tell him he was doing shit.

" No! You can't be too colourful over there. ZA there's a style for everyone. And too colourful isn't for you." Zakhi heard the new nickname Balz had just given him. ZA.

" Oh so I'm not good enough for the tuxedo? What? Am I too ugly for colour" he was just teasing but Balz seemed to take it seriously.

" Oh no.. I didn't mean it like that. You're too Good looking to be called ugly. " His eyes were back to the two tuxedos he was inspecting in his arms.

" You said I'm good looking. " Zakhi got closer to tease him more but as always something broke the moment. This time it was...still Zinzi bumping into him.

" Babe! I didn't know you were coming here. " Zinzi hooked her arm into Zakhi's.

Zakhi thought it was his imagination playing tricks on him when he saw Balz look away with a tear dripping from his left eye but when he saw him wipe it he knew for sure he must have done something to offend Balz again.

God knew he wanted to know what he kept on doing wrong in all of this.

Chapter Five : Red handed

Zinzi got inside her car. Zakhi followed behind her. Balz went to sit at the backseat. That did nothing to smooth Zinzi's worries. It only made them stronger. Zakhi was sitting beside her but his eyes were on the mirror looking at Balz. Balz who looked like the world had defeated him in some ultimate battle. She would have felt bad for her brother if he hadn't made a war with her. Now she would destroy him anyhow she could.

" Zakhi why didn't you take any of the tuxedos I chose for you?" She questioned as she started to drive the car.

Zakhi only sighed looking through the rear mirror. " How can I? Those tuxedos you chose were colourful and someone warned me from wearing anything with too much colour. "

" It seems I'm not good looking enough for them"

Zinzi was about to reply. To say that whoever said that about her boyfriend was downright insane. Her man is so good looking that even trash would look good on him.

" I never said t! I said too colourful things wouldn't work with you but never said you weren't good looking! I totally explained that. " Balz said looking right at Zakhi who had turned to face him.

Zakhi smiled. " Finally I got you to speak. Do you really know how annoying it is for the person who talks too much to just be silent for some reason. And I the person who should be silent had to get you to speak."

Balz folded his hands. Looking away from Zakhi.

" Come on now! Don't be like that. You can't just look away from me when you want to. If you're mad at me say it! I will apologize don't just look away from me!" Zakhi never apologized to Zinzi. Even when she did things to show him how hurt she was. He never cared enough to respond. But here he was begging her brother. Her brother who used to call him names and insulted him. Her brother who he'd call his worst enemy was now the person he'd rather beg to look at him. The one he'd rather listen to fashion advice from. The one that wanted him for himself.

" I'm not angry or mad at you. I never was. The note you wrote wasn't necessary. And what you're doing now isn't necessary. I just... I'm not in the mood right now." With that he turned to his window again.

Zinzi could practically see the desperation in Zakhi's face as he sat correctly. He looked like he was one of those guys that wanted to get back their lost loves or something. That expression above all else drove Zinzi mad. She gripped too hard on the steering wheel. Didn't even notice she had lost the road in her path before she crashed into a tree.

" The hell!" Zakhi exclaimed, " Only I crash cars. What are you doing playing me my dear?"

Zinzi smiled innocently. " Guess you rub on me."

" Well you shouldn't let that happen often. You know how dangerous it is to crash a car. Someone always gets hurt. Good thing though that no one got hurt. Right Balz?" Balz didn't reply.

Zinzi saw the quick change in Zakhi. The playful nature he had just showed disappeared immediately.

" Beu?!" he shouted now looking at Balz's face which had blood prickling out of his forehead. There his side of the window was shattered. Meaning the cause was him smashing his head into it.

" Call for help" Zakhi ordered Zinzi as he got off the car. Rushing to open Balz's door. He shook him but Balz wasn't responding.

Zinzi really felt bad now. She had hurt her brother. She didn't mean to. She really didn't. Her anger just got the worst of her.

" Beu wake up!" Zakhi shook him again this time being successful as Balz sneezed. " Why do you smell like blood?" Zakhi only breathed thankful to whoever God that heard his prayers. He didn't know what he'd do if his Beu would have been hurt severely. Wait..his Beu?

" Don't move. You're bleeding but not as much as I thought. It's probably just going to hurt a lot."

Balz looked at him.

" What?"

" Was that your silly idea to make me feel better? By telling me how it's gonna hurt! Are you even human?"

" Last time I checked. But maybe you could check. "

Balz rolled his eyes. He tried to sit up. The position he was sitting in wasn't comfortable at all. But Zakhi stopped him halfway .

" You'll lose more blood when you move around."

" Nurse's nephew kanene" he muttered softly to himself. Not thinking Zakhi would hear him. But he did hear him.

" I hear you."

" So what? It wasn't like I was hiding it from you. "

" You're gonna regret talking so much once the ambulance is here. " Zakhi warned.

" And what the hell does that mean?" Balz asked being frightened now.

" Well you'll see for yourself. I've seen a lot of people go in an ambulance but never see them get out." Balz bit his lip. He had never been in an ambulance before. To say the truth he couldn't even remember the last time he went to the hospital.

" Are you trying to frighten me? Because if you are it's working. " Zakhi chuckled. " Am I?"

Balz didn't want to die. He didn't want to go in an ambulance and then not get out. " You know what? I think I'm just fine. There's no need for any ambulances. None whatsoever. I will just get home throw a band-aid on that puppy then I'll be all good. "

" Really now?" Zakhi was just trying to play around with Balz he didn't know he'd actually get him scared. But this gave him an idea. " You know if you let me go with you I'd protect you. "

Balz lifted his brow and laughed. " You'd protect me? As in who? My bodyguard?"

" Well it is that I go with you or well... I don't know what will happen" Zakhi looked at Balz who bit his lip with more anxiousness.

" Fine. Just because I don't want to be stolen for kidney transplants. Not because I'm scared!" Zakhi nodded hiding the sly smile he had on for his success.

His aunt would have his ear for lying about the ambulance. His aunt believed that you should appreciate the Lord every single day for the people that work for your well being and health. And he did. His aunt loved helping people so much so that Zakhi wondered why she left her nursing job.

A mystery that would just take time to solve. Time he didn't have. Right now he wanted to see if Balz was hurt or it was just as he said only a scratch.

" Wonder what's taking so long for this ambulance to come. "

Balz growled. " Want me to die already?!"

Zakhi only shook his head. Even when injured Balz was still cantankerous than ever. He was about to go check at Zinzi. He felt guilty that he just only ran to one sibling leaving the one that was his girlfriend alone. It wasn't his fault though. He had no control over his emotions these days. Emotions that favoured Balz above his sister. But when he got out of the car the ambulance was already there.

He could see the fear in Balz as he gulped down. Zakhi really felt bad now. He shouldn't have scared him so much. How would he have known that the sarcastic boy actually did have fears.

" It's okay I'm here aren't I?" he tried to smooth him the best he could. Balz looked at him with an expression that only made Zakhi even more angry at himself for scaring Balz. He just looked so frightened. Like a mouse seeing a cat in front of it. " You're here. You won't leave?" Balz asked softly.

Zakhi held Balz's hand. " I won't leave. I'll never leave you in trouble." He wanted to add or Ever but it would be too weird. This whole thing was already weird on its own.

Two paramedics came to help Balz out. But he refused their help. Zakhi went to try. Balz agreed to his help.

They reached the ambulance. Where Balz was placed on the stretcher. He kept his eyes only on Zakhi. Zakhi who looked very worried.

" Are you okay?" Balz wanted to speak and argue with Zakhi for being a fool of course he was okay. He was here with him. He had said it himself. If he was with him nothing would happen to him.

His eyes started to get heavy. He tried to fight off the urge to close them just to look at Zakhi. He felt a strong hand on his. The hand that fit his so perfectly. The hand that was so warm.

" Sleep" Zakhi ordered. He wanted to whine and be argumentative but he saw himself already in the world of darkness only meaning he had fallen asleep.

M ax and Josh excitedly looked at each other.
" Yes! It's working. Just a few more steps and then lift off. " Said a overexcited Max.

Josh only smiled at his mate. It was great looking at him happy. Than angry at him. For a crime he wasn't even at fault for. He'd make it his mission to fix everything that was broken between his mate and himself. But now they had to finish this mission.

" We should get her to her car before she wakes up. " He said looking at the unconscious Zinzi on the ground. They had to sting her. If they didn't she would have ruined everything.

" Yeah, you sure she won't remember us stinging her right?" Max asked with an concerned look in his eyes. Which just served to annoy Josh.

What was this girl to his mate? That he'd even worry if she saw them sting her. He wanted to say that. But he didn't want to make Max more angrier than he already was.

" No, she won't remember"

Balz woke up in a hospital room. Just the sounds of the machines alone scared him. Along with all the things Zakhi had told him he was shivering now.

" Hey,welcome to the world of the living. " He twisted his head to the side to see the fool on a couch next to his bed.

" You do know that you could sprain your neck like that. " Zakhi scolded as he got up from his seat and went to place Balz's head on the pillows.

" Wa—wawwetter" he didn't think Zakhi would understand since he himself wasn't understanding himself either.

He felt a glass press up to his lips. " Drink" Zakhi told him. He drank the water filling his thirst. Zakhi pulled away the glass from Balz's lips. " You need more?"

Balz shook his head. Since he didn't trust his mouth to speak hearable words. He felt the side of the bed dip. Then he felt Zakhi's hand on his shoulder. Moving him closer to him.

He wanted to ask Zakhi why he was doing that. Why he was snuggling him so close to him but he found that he couldn't. Not because of his momentarily flawed speech but because he also wanted to be close to Zakhi.

" Beu, I think I'm going mad. I don't know what's happening to me. If I'm being weird or anything forgive me but I can't stop myself" he didn't understand what Zakhi was saying but he sure liked the feeling from warm arms that grasped his body. Zakhi kept on pushing them both close together. So close that it felt like they were being tangled together,the tangle became even more as he decided to help out as well by wrapping his legs around Zakhi.

" We're so closely linked yet I can't feel you. And I want to feel you" he confessed feeling no embarrassment or shame in the words. Zakhi held his hand to Balz's lips. " Maybe we aren't doing it right"

" How do we do it right?" How was this even right? They had forgotten all about right or wrong and normal all what they cared about now was what they were feeling right now. And what they were feeling was automatically generated to sexual frustration. They wanted more from each other. So much more.

Zakhi kissed Balz gently. Balz didn't want it that way. He had been waiting far too long for their kiss and their touches that he didn't want gentle. He wanted rough,he wanted passion. So he grabbed the back of Zakhi's head pulling him even more to himself. The kiss heated up even more as they roughly kissed each other. Their passion went on overdrive.

Zakhi had never felt this kind of feeling for anybody. He had never kissed none of the girls he had dated like this. Not even Zinzi. Balz's injuries long forgotten as they rolled around the small hospital bed. Hands were starting to reach under both their shirts when they were interrupted by a loud gasp.

They didn't feel like breaking apart. They didn't want to break apart. Instead of separating or breaking apart they just continued kissing feeling each other.

With even more fierce passion. The person would just have to go and come back

" Zakhi! Get off my brother!" Oh no...Zinzi! Why was she here? How was she here? They had left her. " I don't believe this! I knew it! I knew you both were not as before! I knew you both were not what you pretended to be! Oh my God!" she screamed pacing the room.

Zakhi tried to make himself care enough to let Balz free from his hold. But he couldn't. Right now he wasn't caring he only was feeling.

" Balz! Unwrap your legs from my boyfriend!" Her screaming didn't help nothing. Zakhi didn't get off Balz and Balz didn't unwrap his legs just tightened them even more around Zakhi.

Just looking the position made Zinzi angry and disgusted. She fumed with anger. And stomped out of the hospital room.

Never had she felt so abused. So betrayed and hurt. How could they? How could Zakhi? Where did she go wrong we a girlfriend?

She wasn't perfect. But she couldn't have been so wrong that Zakhi and Balz would betray her like this. How could she go on? She'd be a laughing stock at school. Just thinking about it made her head hurt. How insulted she felt right now.

To have caught her own brother with her boyfriend in a hospital room! How could life be so cruel?

Chapter Six : Drink away the pain

BALZ WAS MOANING AS Zakhi licked at his exposed chest. The wet tongue drove him to madness. Especially when Zakhi went and bit down on his nipple. Balz's nipples have always been sensitive even the brush of air made them tingle. But what Zakhi was doing now wasn't causing tingles it was causing something else entirely.

Zakhi's tongue went lower exploring the whole other Balz's upper body. While his right hand had sneaked itself inside Balz's jeans.

Pumping Balz's cock. Balz screamed at the instant pleasure that brought him. " ZAaaamhhhm!" he held on the bed's sheets as he felt his organism on the brink of the edge. Zakhi's face went to the side of his shoulder. Going straight to the neck. He felt Zakhi bite down on it.

That was his undoing. Along with the pumping on his cock he couldn't take it anymore he screamed as he went to his release. " Ahhh.." he closed his eyes as he felt all his energy fall out of him.

He felt Zakhi fall beside him. When he turned to look at Zakhi's direction he saw that he was the only one that benefited from Zakhi's touches. He guilty looked at Zakhi's still high up proud erection.

He didn't know how to pleasure anyone. It was the result of not being in any relationship for all of his life. His only sexual experience was the one he didn't want to remember. He had swore to himself that after what his cousin did to him he'd never be able to trust or to love someone enough to have a relationship with.

And then Zakhi had to complicate things with making him fall for him. And now he was thinking of ways to pleasure him. How did Zakhi even know to do what he did? Last time he checked Zakhi wasn't gay. And then how would he know how to pleasure another man? Like he did a few seconds ago.

" Why do you always overthink everything?" he heard Zakhi's voice ask him. Why did he? He didn't know..he just did.

" Why don't you think things at all?"

" What's there to think about?" Zakhi asked casually as if nothing had happened. As if laying next to a guy who was naked and he'd just pumped was normal.

" Everything. Zakhi you do realize what we have just done? You do know that my sister saw us right? Your girlfriend caught you red handed making out with her brother. Doesn't that bother you even a little?" he asked himself the same question and wished it did bother him. Wished that he did feel ashamed for moaning so hard under his sister's boyfriend.

" So?" he didn't just hear Zakhi ask that. He could be insensitive and not understand other people's pains but not Zakhi.

" Why would you say that? She's your girlfriend! You should be feeling guilty or running after her or something but this calm thing you're doing now." He sat up ready to take his clothes from the floor. But Zakhi stopped him.

" Are you really angry at me now?" He said pulling Balz to face him. " What did I do wrong? I told you I don't know what's happening to me. That I'm getting mad. And the only thing that seems make me sane is you." He held Balz's hand to his. " I was so confused. I went crazy when you were hurt, I couldn't sleep without finding out if you slept. I just couldn't do anything that didn't include you. And then I finally got it. I got the reason"

" What's the reason?" Balz questioned.

" The reason is simple. It's that I've fallen in love with you. I know it's wrong to fall in love with your girlfriend's brother but you can't control what you feel. Now can you?"

Balz shook his head. He knew more than anyone that he couldn't control his emotions. He still felt like kissing Zakhi all over again that just showed how much of a bad brother he was. Sure he and Zinzi didn't really get along. Which siblings do? But what they didn't do was steal one's boyfriend. And this looked like he had just done that.

Zakhi must have seen his sunken face, he lifted his chin up. " Hey it's nothing to be ashamed about. It's nothing to feel ashamed about. It's life. We can't stop it. And we can't stop what we're feeling now."

" But what about Zinzi?" Zakhi sighed looking at Balz. " I don't know, I really don't know. But right now I don't want to think about that. I have a hard-on and want to take care of that. "

Balz's eyes instinctively went to Zakhi's crotch that still was hidden by his jeans. He bit his lip. " How come I'm the only one naked?"

Zakhi smiled. " Because you're the only one who wanted them off. "

" Okay...well now I want yours off now" Balz commanded with a voice trying to be brave for this.

" Beu you do know you don't have to do anything right? I'm fine"

No this was the first time someone actually said they loved him. This was the first time someone had cared enough to pleasure him than himself. He needed to pay that back.

" I want to do something. Something to please you" he tugged at Zakhi's shirt but before he could unbutton it Zakhi had both his hands. Kissing them fondly. " You generous idiot."

" You shouldn't be agreeing so soon to please me. I'm a beast in the sack.. even though I say that myself. I just have to warn you. It's still too soon for that. I don't want to hurt you—yet"

" Why do you frighten me Zakhi?" Balz playfully asked as he took both his hands away from Zakhi's hold.

" It's just fun I guess. " Zakhi brushed Balz's hair out of his face. " We've got to go home now. I'm sure the hospital staff has heard enough of us already" that made Balz's face to immediately go red. He was so embarrassed. What did the doctors,nurses and patients think of him?

" I didn't say that to make you feel bad you know. I really appreciate your foul mouth. I wonder what's it's gonna do when I actually fuck you" Zakhi whispered in Balz's ear. He didn't know where all this new character of himself came from but he liked it. And liked seeing how Balz flushed and got all red.

Balz finally got himself free from Zakhi and went to find his clothes which were scattered everywhere in the room. He found his shirt and jeans along with his shoes what was missing was his boxers.

Zakhi's amused chuckle surprised him and made him to turn looking at him. Only to see Zakhi holding the boxers with his left hand. " Looking for this?"

He snatched it angrily huffing. Zakhi so didn't act like himself right now!

They were walking out of the room. Balz kept on looking on the ground than at the people around them. He was too afraid to look at them. The judging looks were not what he wanted to see. And he knew he'd get them from all the people.

" Hiding your eyes won't make them go away. You know right? Better face your fears than hide from them my dear" Zakhi said raising his chin. " Why would you hide such pretty eyes?"

" Zakhi stop it. Let's go." Balz didn't like attention drawn to him especially not when it was about his sexuality. His sexuality was always a very sensitive issue to him. He never really identified it. It was too hard and painful for him to do.

Zakhi didn't speak anymore until they walked out of the hospital. It was the only time Balz breathed out a sigh.

" Beu those people weren't even looking at us. You were paranoid" Zakhi informed him with a voice that told him Zakhi was now concerned.

" Whether they were looking or they weren't I don't care. As long as we're out of there now. All I need right now is a shower and some sleep. " Balz said as he and Zakhi began to walk.

" Which house are we going to?" Balz frowned at the weird question Zakhi just asked him.

" Well.. your house is closer so we'll leave each other there."

Zakhi's expression changed immediately at hearing that. " So you want to walk alone? In this lonely night. Not happening. It's either you come to my house and spend the night or I come to yours"

" Why?"

Zakhi sighed softly to himself. The kind of bad luck he had to be the only smart one in the world. " You're injured Beu. I have to be there to nurse you back to health"

" No you don't. I can always be better without you. It's not like it's that much of a wound. I can't wait for it to heal. This bandage on my forehead is not a good look on me. "

" I think you look Alright. "

Balz smiled and stopped their walking. " Of caurse you'd say that. Who wouldn't say that to a person who he just fell in love with?" the last part made him blush. Fallen in love. Zakhi was actually in love with him..he wasn't forced into something he didn't want to. Instead just given the time to take his own pace.

He loved that Zakhi understood how he was feeling. Liked that he didn't make him feel uncomfortable because of his past or disappointed. Zakhi just became Zakhi.

" Of caurse I would but Beu you're beautiful there's no need for me to lie about that." Balz didn't know how much he'd survive Zakhi's compliments and teases. " Now come on it's getting even more darker by the second. "

Zakhi took his hand. Dragging him along the road. Zakhi had always been a fast person while walking so this was not a new thing for Balz. But it didn't mean he could keep up. Not at Zakhi's pace. He wobbled and tripped over a rock.

He hissed under his breath not wanting to alert Zakhi. But he did anyway. Zakhi's eyes roamed to his. " What happened? Are you in pain?"

He shook his head. His head injuries were a forgotten problem to him. His leg at moment was throbbing. " No, I'm not. It's just you walk too fast. " Zakhi gave him an apologizing look. " Sorry, I'm not used with walking with someone." Balz was seeing a lot of different sides to Zakhi today. Sides he'd not cared to see or acknowledge at the time. Zakhile is caring, loving, a little too possessive along with being extremely sexy as hell.

" It's okay let's just go at a slower pace now. Okay?" Zakhi nodded. They walked slowly even more slower since Balz sprained his ankle. Zakhi kept on looking at him. " It wasn't your fault. I tripped over a damn rock"

" But you wouldn't have tripped if I had been more careful. I should have known not to walk so fast with you. " Zakhi said clearly regretting his mistake.

" Can I kiss you?" Balz asked suddenly getting out of context. Zakhi's face turned from guilty to straight up evilly smirking.

" You wanna kiss me?" he asked Balz who nodded bravely. Only increasing Zakhi's smirk. " Why?"

Balz didn't know how to reply to this. He just wanted to stop Zakhi from his stupid guilt tripping and he just wanted to feel Zakhi's lips against his. There was no explanation needed for this. It just had to be felt. That is why he decided to ignore Zakhi's question and leaned for the kiss anyway. He didn't care that they were out in the public. Didnt care if people would be looking or talking about them the next day. All he cared about at this moment was the boy in front of him. The boy that had his heart. The boy that he had called so many names..the only name he wanted to call him now was Lover.

He didn't seem to care about his sister who would be hurt even more about this. He didn't seem to care about his parents. What their views and opinions about this would be no.. right now he only wanted to be Zakhi's. Right now he only wanted to be with Zakhi.

Their kiss wasn't gentle, neither was it rough. It was just right. The way their lips blended together was something out of this world. The way their tongues explored each other's mouths was both enticing and fascinating. They couldn't get enough of each other. That was the problem. They had forgotten they were outside,in a stranded road where anyone could see them. Neither did they care.

Balz fumbled with Zakhi's shirt. Unbuttoning it but when he was midway Zakhi's hand stopped him. Pulling himself away from their passion fueled kiss. Balz let out a whine at the loss of the other's warm mouth and soft lips. " You don't want to do that" this was the second time today Zakhi was warning him. At first he had listened because he was afraid. But not now. Now he wasn't afraid. He wanted this...he needed this.

" Zakhile please don't refuse me. Not now. I want you inside me right now. I want you inside me. Do not hesitate or think about it. That's what you said right? Don't think about it. Feel" Zakhi still didn't want to hurt Balz in anyway. That's why he was being so hesitant. He didn't want Balz to regret it.

But the little guy in between his legs had other plans. Balz took that as an advantage. As he brushed his kneecap on it . " Don't starve yourself" he said at the most seductive voice he could muster. He knew he was acting like a little slut in heat right but no one could blame him. This would be his first time being with someone who he really wanted to be intimate with.

" What the heck" Zakhi said as he attacked Balz with a kiss. A kiss that wasn't like their last one but an even more firesome passion.

They helped each other with removing their clothes. Throwing them on the pavement.

Balz lay on the madeshift bed which was their clothes on the ground. He watched as Zakhi went on top of him. " Are you sure?" he asked in the most serious tone Balz had ever heard him speak with.

Balz's eyes closed. Automatically going to the memories he had been raped by his cousin. The memories of him screaming for help. The pain he had felt afterwards. Not just physically but also emotionally. That experience had completely traumatized his whole being. Making him lose everything he ever believed in. His trust and his heart were broken. In the worst kind of way possible.

He opened his eyes again. Looking at the one on top of him. Zakhi had no forceful intentions towards him. Zakhile was the one who was still asking him if he was sure about them making love even though he had heard Balz ask it himself. Zakhi was the one who looked at him now with concern in his eyes.

" Yes, yes I am sure. Now stop stalling and just fuck me" Zakhi didn't have to be asked twice as he got to work immediately.

Zinzi was sitting in a bar. What was she doing here again? Oh yeah...she saw the two people she loved in this world betray her. They didn't even have the sense of at least apologizing. No! They didn't even acknowledge her existence. Just kept on with their kissing. She wouldn't be surprised even if they were somewhere now have intense sex.

What got her the most was that she didn't even know what she had done wrong. As a girlfriend and a sister. Zakhi and her always seemed happy. They never fought more than a normal couple would. They never cheated on each other. Zakhi never gave Zinzi reason to. And Zinzi didn't give any to Zakhi. Because they worked together in real life and in the bedroom. They were in love....or so she thought.

Balz and her had usual sibling rivalry. Nothing more than what it should be. Nothing that they couldn't get over with. Nothing so painful and hurting. Nothing as this at all.

Now she was in a bar. A place she had previously hated because this was where people's lives were wasted. This was the place people's father's monies were finished. But today this was the place that she would drink away the pain. The pain that she felt hurting in her chest.

The pain she knew would be healed by time but not now. Not at this moment. She couldn't be forgiving or forgetful right now. She was pitying herself too much.

Chapter Seven: She'd pay

Josh came in the bedroom. Where Max lay down on his back. Eyes looking at the roof. It was now or never. It was either he spoke now he would have to let himself die silently every single day. With seeing his Max looking at him with disgusted eyes or with confused expressions. It was today that he'd explain and tell Max everything. It was today that he had to fix his relationship with his mate.

" You should talk. You'll explode if you stand like that for a long time" Max said still looking at the roof. He was moody. Just one of the side effects to the pregnancy. Which would be more than any mood swings he'd ever experienced since these were three babies. Three whole babies.

He was excited but also afraid too. Especially to lose them. If he lost these children he wouldn't be able to have other children. Not that his body would have any problem with it but it would be his soul. He couldn't stand being the one to drip blood out instead of giving birth to his children.

He couldn't stand that Josh never knew the pain he caused to him every time that happened. Every time that silent pain went to him. He wanted to feel all of these moments of the pregnancy with his mate. His chosen one. His forever,his every life time but he was afraid that if he trusted Josh again he'd hurt him as he did every time.

He was afraid of losing these children and he was afraid of losing the last hope he had on his mate. If this one broke he would rather kill himself than be tortured all over again knowing that his mate was cheating on him with his sister.

" Sandra was at fault not I" Josh started catching Max's attention. "
She was the one who forced me to do all of those things. Believe me if I
knew that...you were carrying our children all those times I would have
tried harder to fight her"

Max didn't believe this. Instead of Josh admitting his mistakes and
apologize so they could try and go back to the normal them. He just
put more blame to his sister. " How was Sandra the only one at fault?
Yes she knew that you and I were mates and should have been more of
a loyal sister and kept herself far from my man but you have the same
amount..if not more blame. You knew how cheating hurts our mating
bond. You knew that you weren't supposed to cheat! You came every
single night after you were done with my sister to fuck me! What? Were
you comparing who was better? What did you get?! Was I worse? That
you had to shame me in worst possible way! You didn't just sleep with my
sister but you came and slept with me too. Just moments after I'd felt you
finish with Sandra. Who do you think you are?!"

Josh could hear the anger, the agony and sadness in Max's tone. It
teared at him. " Max calm down"

Max got up the bed. Walking straight to Josh shoving him to the
wall. " I will not calm down! Why should I? To protect the babies?
They'll probably die too because you'll cheat on me just the first moment
you lay your eyes on Sandra. You know I should just make it easier for
you. I'll kill myself right here. So my babies and I can die at least on our
terms! So at least..." he broke down crying. His fists beating Josh's chest.
And Josh took all the beating. If it was what would make Max feel better
then he'd be a punching bag.

" What did I do wrong?! What didn't I do? What was my fault?
Why! Why did you have to betray me? Not just cheat but cheating with
my blood...my sister. How will I be able to see you two together now? Do
you know how difficult it was for me to keep myself busy with everything
just to ignore your infidelity? I love you...you son of a Arktid!"

He stopped hitting Josh. Breathing heavily to catch his breath.

" She drugged me. The first time she drugged me. The second time she threatened to tell the council about us. You know what the council would have done to you. They would have labeled you as a traitor and had you hanged. I didn't want that. I loved you too much to let you die. I knew it would hurt you..but I had to sleep with her to make sure you were safe. I really didn't know that you were pregnant and getting pregnant all that time. If I knew I know that I would have fought more for us. " Max stood there. Unable to understand a word Josh said.

" I didn't cheat on purpose or anything of the sort. There's absolutely nothing wrong with you. There never was. I came to sleep with you every night after I had slept with her because I didn't knot on her and I wanted to keep the knot just for you. As it should be. I was stupid not to know that would have gotten you pregnant a long time ago. I was stupid and insane. Please forgive me. I... I"

Max saw his mate fall to the ground. He rushed to him. " Josh!" he screamed as he saw the mark on his neck. " Oh no" he shook his head as he knew exactly what this meant. Josh was telling the truth. He wasn't to be blamed for all the miscarriages. He wasn't the one that cheated on him. The person who was to be blamed was his sister. She was the one responsible for all his pain.

And she'd pay. She'd pay for everything she had done to him. She'd pay. For what she'd done to his Josh now. She'd pay. He didn't care that the council would probably kill him at first whim of the children inside of him but he cared for Josh's life. He wouldn't let his mate die. Not like this. Never like this.

Next-Part Three: Never Ever

About The Book

BALZ AND ZAKHI ARE faced with two impossible choices - leave the only world they've ever known, or stay and face the cruelty that has surrounded them for so long. As they struggle to decide their fate, they must come to terms with the challenges that life has thrown at them. Can they find the strength to move forward, or will they be trapped in a cycle of despair? Find out in this gripping third part to "I AM HUMAN TOO," where the stakes have never been higher.

If you love books that explore the human experience in all its complexity, then you'll want to read "I AM HUMAN TOO: NEVER EVER." Filled with drama and emotion, this novel is sure to keep you reading until the very last page. So pick up your copy today and prepare for an unforgettable journey!

Author's Thanks

Hey you! My goodness you've got no idea what this means to me. You're the best.

And I want you to know that.

It's stars like you that keep authors like me going strong.

Without a reader what's a writer?

Always remember that you are the important one and you are the star.

Hope you enjoyed my book and that you're looking forward for more or already heading to some of mine as we speak.

Now Star please do me two big favours rate my book tell me what you liked about it. Tell me what you didn't like but please don't be harsh my heart is made of glass it breaks fast.

Again thank you for reading! And have a good day.

Ane M

Don't miss out!

Visit the website below and you can sign up to receive emails whenever Ane M publishes a new book. There's no charge and no obligation.

https://books2read.com/r/B-A-KYHJ-OEORC

Connecting independent readers to independent writers.

Did you love *I Am Human Too: My Blood*? Then you should read *I Am Human Too: Never Ever*[1] by Ane M!

Balz and Zakhi are faced with two impossible choices - leave the only world they've ever known, or stay and face the cruelty that has surrounded them for so long. As they struggle to decide their fate, they must come to terms with the challenges that life has thrown at them. Can they find the strength to move forward, or will they be trapped in a cycle of despair? Find out in this gripping third part to "I AM HUMAN TOO," where the stakes have never been higher.

If you love books that explore the human experience in all its complexity, then you'll want to read "I AM HUMAN TOO: NEVER EVER." Filled with drama and emotion, this novel is sure to keep you

---

1. https://books2read.com/u/bzvyPZ

2. https://books2read.com/u/bzvyPZ

reading until the very last page. So pick up your copy today and prepare for an unforgettable journey!

Also by Ane M

Billionaire For The Holidays
Billionaire For The Holidays

The Love games
I Am Human Too (Rain Again)
I Am Human Too: My Blood
I Am Human Too: Never Ever
I Am Yours: Love In Full Bloom
I Am Yours: Between The Lines

About the Author

You're crazy! It will never happen..they all said not knowing that it is what I am aiming for. A surprise. A unsual kind of book. Books that are only loved by people who understand what not understanding is. A book that's for all of us who love romances. No matter how young the person might be love is love.